THREE HORSES

Clover Fields Fiasco

A 4D BOOK

by Cari Meister

illustrated by Heather Burns

PICTURE WINDOW BOOKS
a capstone imprint

Three Horses is published by Picture Window Books,
A Capstone Imprint
1710 Roe Crest Drive
North Mankato, Minnesota 56003
www.mycapstone.com

Library of Congress Cataloging-in-Publication Data is available
on the Library of Congress website.
ISBN: 978-1-5158-2947-8 (library binding)
ISBN: 978-1-5158-2951-5 (paperback)
ISBN: 978-1-5158-2955-3 (eBook PDF)

Designer:
Lori Bye

Design elements by Shutterstock: Semiletava Hanna

Printed and boudn in the USA
PA017

Download the Capstone  app!

- Ask an adult to download the Capstone 4D app.

- Scan the cover and stars inside the book for additional content.

When you scan a spread, you'll find
fun extra stuff to go with this book!
You can also find these things
on the web at www.capstone4D.com
using the password: threehorses.29478

TABLE OF CONTENTS

CHAPTER 1
The Barn Cat That Is Really a Horse.....5

CHAPTER 2
The Blizzard. 12

CHAPTER 3
Escape!. 17

CHAPTER 4
Tres Caballos Incognito. 22

CHAPTER 5
The Big Dark Something 29

CHAPTER 6
The Clover Field. 34

CHAPTER 7
Stuck 40

CHAPTER 8
The Rescue. 44

CHAPTER 9
Back at the Barn 49

CHAPTER 1

The Barn Cat That Is Really a Horse

"Sleep well, Princess," said Melody sliding the stall door closed. "I'll see you in the morning."

Melody dropped a handful of carrots in Princess' bucket and skipped down the barn aisle.

Princess nosed the bucket and huffed in disgust.

"Why, oh why does she give me carrots?" Princess snorted. She pawed the ground.

"Doesn't she know cats like tuna or cheese? But every day it is the same. Carrots, carrots, carrots!" Princess continued.

Sebastian, the big draft horse, sniffed through the stall bars.

"What do you want?" asked Princess.

Seb's big brown eyes darted to her bucket.

"Oh, yes. Of course," said Princess. "The carrots."

Princess picked up the carrots with her teeth and pushed them through the stall bars.

"Here you go, Seb. I know how much horses like carrots. I, on the other hand, want something more fitting a feline's fondness."

Seb looked Princess up and down. Nope. She hadn't changed. She was still the same perfect palomino pony she always was.

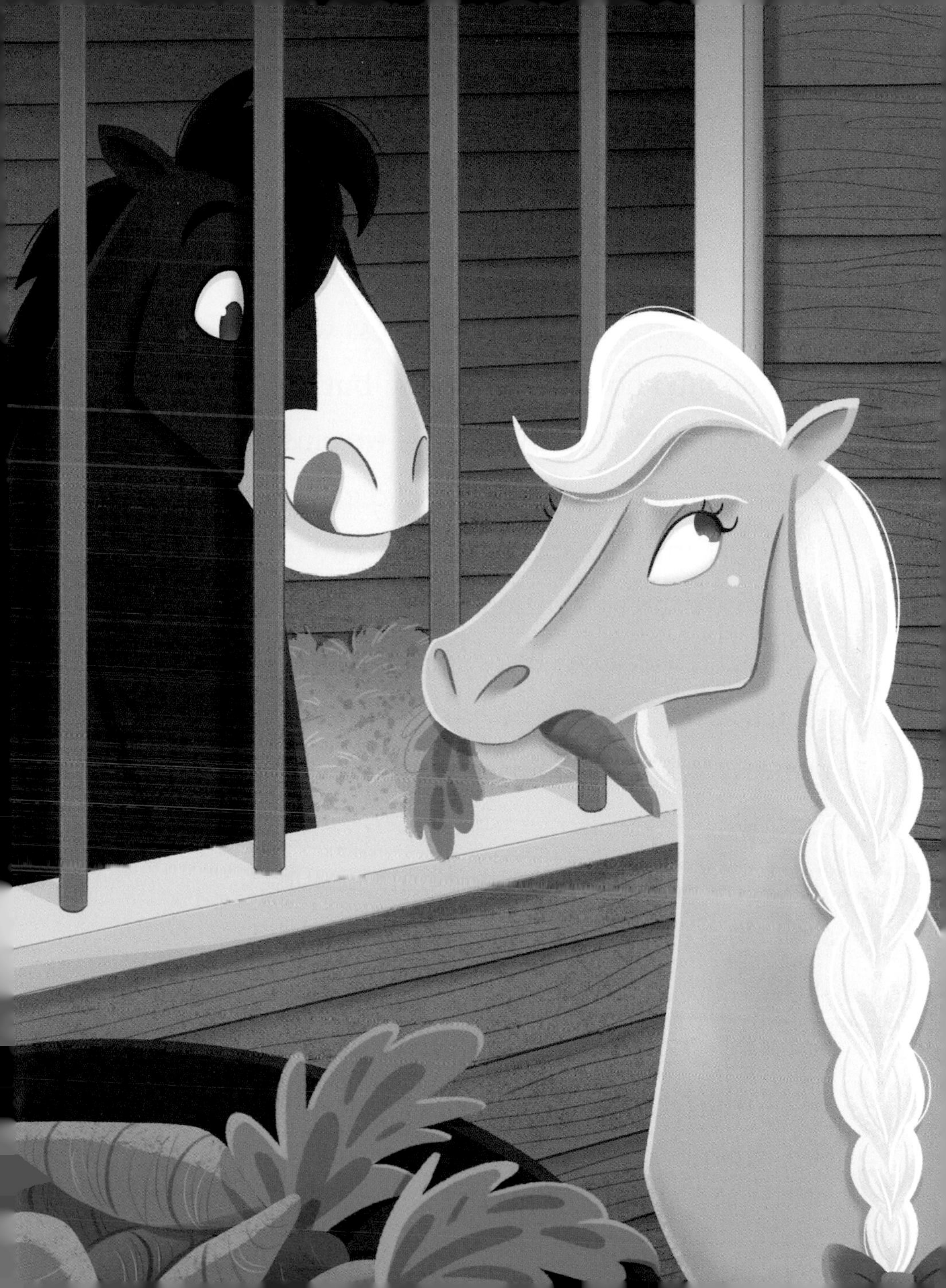

Tonight, Melody had brushed and braided Princess' mane. She had added a bright pink bow. Princess' hooves had been painted with sparkly polish.

Every horse knew that Princess was the most spoiled horse in the barn, but Princess didn't seem to care. When she was just a newborn foal, her mother had died. A stray cat came into her stall and had kittens. To this day, Princess truly, unmistakably, 100% believed she was a cat.

Seb crunched on the carrots and watched Princess lick her legs with her long horse tongue.

"I hope I don't get a fur ball tonight!" said Princess. "I just hate that!"

Seb didn't say anything. He never tried to talk Princess out of her crazy delusion. After all, he always got her carrots. Besides, Seb was not one that criticized other horses.

Deep down inside, he knew all horses had special secret dreams . . . and well, if Princess wanted to believe she was a cat, that was her business.

Princess pawed the ground again. "Let me out!" she said. "A barn cat must hunt at night!" Princess kicked the stall. She meowed very loudly. (Well, she thought she meowed, but to all other ears, it came out as a loud whinny.)

Toni, the barn manager, hollered from Snowy's stall. "Settle down, Princess! I'm coming!" She rolled the wheelbarrow full of hay down the aisle toward Princess.

Hay! Again! How disgusting! thought Princess. *If I don't get out of here again tonight, I will not be able to hunt, and I will be forced to eat that dried old stuff just to survive. Oh, the shame! The humiliation! A cat eating hay?*

Wait a minute. I am a cat! Cats are sneaky.
Perhaps I can just sneak right out of the stall
when Toni opens my door. Here she comes.
Princess pawed in excitement.

"Yes, Princess," said Toni. "I won't forget
you!" Princess nuzzled Toni with her head.
Then she tried to push her way out. But Toni
was too fast and too experienced with horses
to let her sneak by.

"Oh no you don't," said Toni pushing her back in. "Eat your hay like a good girl. You have a show tomorrow." She patted her on the neck.

Toni put the wheelbarrow away and shut off the lights. "Good night," she called. "See you in the morning."

Several of the horses neighed good night. But not Princess.

CHAPTER 2

The Blizzard

"Show tomorrow! Show tomorrow! How humiliating!" said Princess. "How ridiculous putting a cat in a horse show! Just imagine how that looks! How can Melody do that to me? When will she see that I am NOT a horse to be led around! I am a cat—a feline wonder."

Most of the other horses were too busy munching on their dinner to pay any attention to Princess' ramblings. But not Snowy. He was just as determined to get out of the barn as Princess was.

Snowy whinnied to Princess.

"What do you want, Snowy?" called Princess.

"Please," said Snowy, "I prefer not to be called that. It does NOT suit me. Call me The Blizzard. After all, that is my show name. Snowy is merely a silly barn name that my owner gave me when he was 3 years old."

Princess stifled a giggle. Snowy was a little Shetland pony—very furry and quite fat. He was cute, for sure. But to call him The Blizzard—a name that makes you think of fear and strength—made Princess chuckle.

"Oh, *pardon moi!*" said Princess. "The Blizzard, what is it you need?"

"I hear you want to get out of here," said Snowy. "And so do I. I've been stuck in here for too long. I am running out of material for my novel."

"You're writing a novel?" asked Princess.

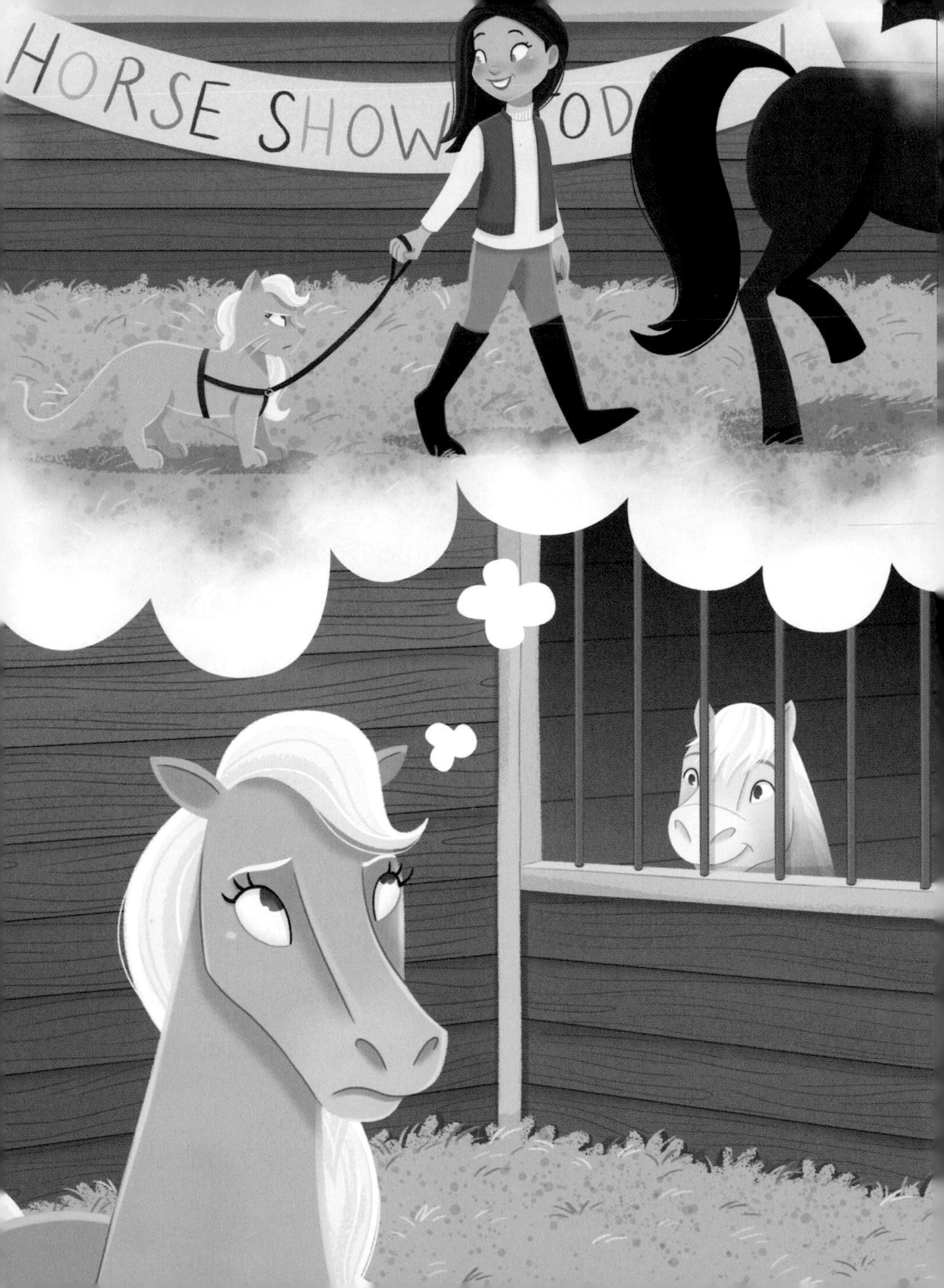
HORSE SHOW

"Yes, of course," said Snowy. "A truly remarkable masterpiece called *From the Horse's Mouth*."

Princess had never heard of a horse writing a novel before. "Oh," she replied.

"Yes," said Snowy. "I need to get out and explore the world. Of course we would come back by morning for breakfast, but I need an adventure! Oh, and I need to find a library to check out a few things."

"I need to get out of this ridiculous stall and explore the night—like a real cat!" said Princess. "Let's go—but wait! How do we get out?"

"We kick our way out!" said Snowy.

CHAPTER 3

Escape!

KICK! STAMP! KICK! KICK! STAMP!

Snowy stopped to catch his breath.
He inspected the wall. No breakthrough.
Not even a dent. Maybe his plan wouldn't
really work . . . but it just HAD to work.
He continued to **KICK, KICK, KICK!**

Princess kicked too.

"What are you doing?" asked Seb.

"Trying to break out!" said Princess.

"Why don't you just stick your head
through, like this?" asked Seb.

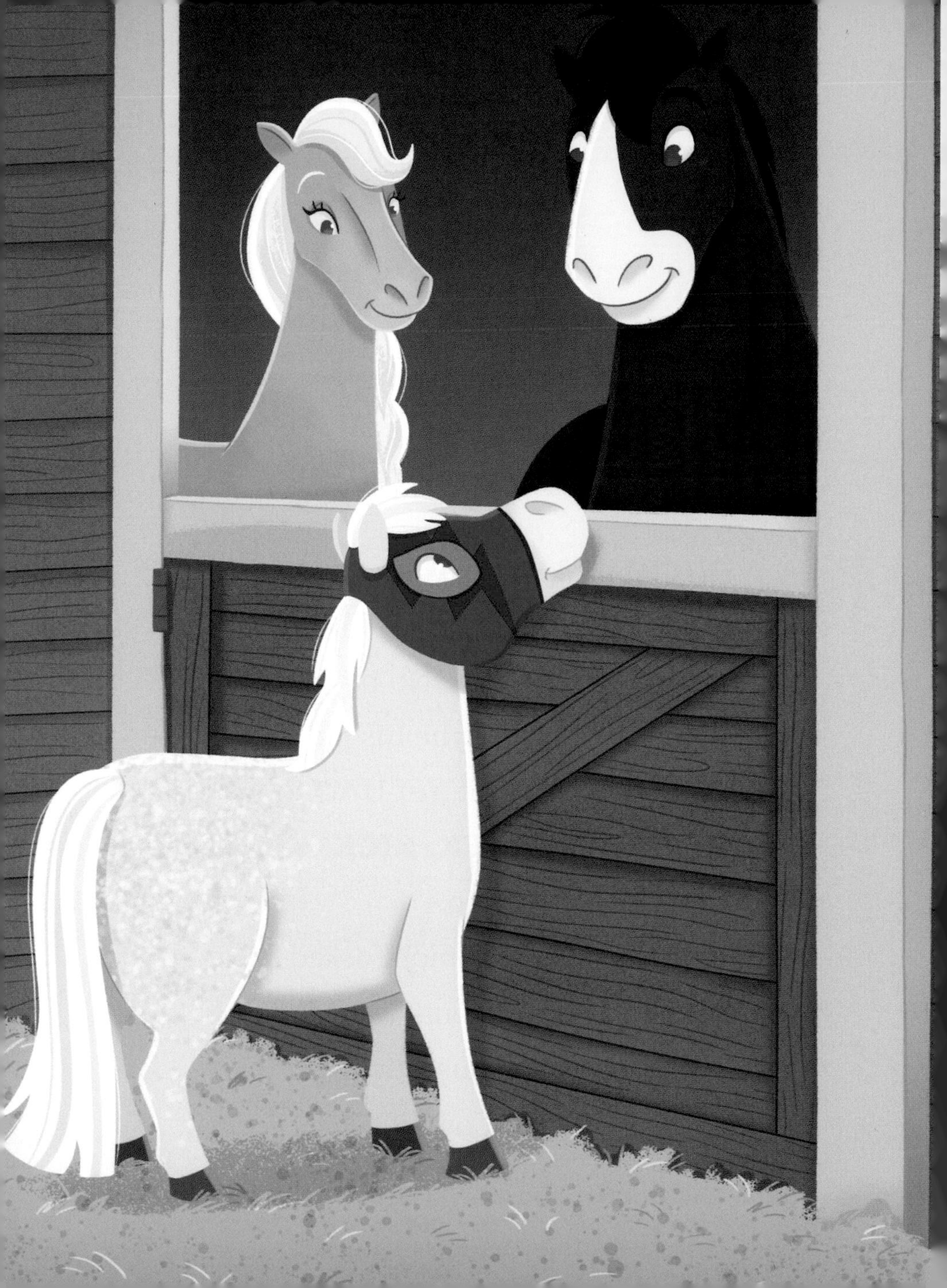

"OK," said Princess.

"Open the latch with your teeth, and walk out . . . like this," Seb told her.

Sebastian was standing in the aisle.

"Meow!" said Princess. "You can't expect a little cat to open that big latch! Can you do it for me?"

Sebastian opened Princess' stall. Princess ran out.

Snowy heard the two horses and stopped kicking. He tried to look out of his stall, but he was not quite tall enough.

"What's going on?" Snowy asked.

"We're free!" said Princess.

"C'mon Seb," said Princess, "Let The Blizzard out! He's writing a novel and needs an adventure!"

"Who?" asked Seb.

"Me!" whinnied Snowy. "The Blizzard!"

Seb smiled. "Oh, you."

He clomped down the aisle, with Princess not far behind.

Seb looked into Snowy's stall. What was that on his face? It looked like a fly mask.

"Are you OK?" asked Princess.

"I'm fine!" said Snowy. "This is my *incognito* mask."

"Your what?" asked Princess.

"My disguise!" said Snowy. "That way, if I'm spotted, no one can tell who I am!"

Seb looked Snowy over. He was still the small, furry, fat Shetland pony—only tonight, he was wearing a fly mask with extra flair. But Seb wasn't going to be the one to tell Snowy that his body was a dead giveaway.

"Here," said Snowy. "I have a few extra. You both should wear them too."

"Me?" asked Seb.

Snowy nodded. "I believe you will prove
yourself a valuable member. After all, look
how crafty you are with latches."

Seb stood up a bit taller and smiled.
It felt good to be included.

CHAPTER 4

Tres Caballos Incognito

After Seb and Princess got their masks on, the three horses looked in the barn mirror.

Seb tilted his head. "We look—"

"Mysterious!" shouted Snowy. "Now all we need is a name."

"A name?" asked Princess.

"Yes!" said Snowy. "We're a posse, and all posses have code names." Snowy tapped his hoof in a thinking kind of way. "I know!" he said. "We will be *Tres Caballos Incognito*!"

Seb blinked. "What does that mean?" he asked.

"*Tres caballos* is Spanish for 'three horses'.
And *incognito* means we are in disguise."

And with that, *Tres Caballos Incognito*
clicked down the aisle, ready for their first
adventure.

They were not too far from the door when
Princess spotted a mouse. She meowed and
meowed (well, huffed and snorted) and
galloped after the mouse. The mouse
ran under the door.

"Open it! Open it!" yelled Princess. "I need my dinner!"

"Wait," said Snowy. "We need a plan. First, we are horses."

Princess shot him a nasty look.

"Oh, and I mean . . . well . . . um, a cat," said Snowy, now looking at Seb. "We are herd animals, so we must stick together. It's safer. We can help each other spot danger and rescue each other if necessary."

Sebastian's big brown eyes grew. "Rescue each other from what?" he asked.

Snowy thought for a minute while Princess sniffed around the barn looking for another mouse. "Wild animals, cars, plastic bags . . . " replied Snowy.

Seb and Princess nodded. Plastic bags blowing in the wind were indeed VERY SCARY. Not only were they unpredictable in their flight, they made noise.

Seb was about to open the barn door when Princess tried to push through.

"Wait!" said Snowy. "We must stick together. You can't just push through. Have some manners!"

"Well, I'm hungry!" said Princess. "I need to hunt! Then after I eat my fill, I'd like a little cat nap."

Just then, Snowy pulled a laptop out from behind the barn door. He picked up a hoof pick with his lips and began typing:

`Princess: hunt.`

"Where did you get that?" asked Seb.

"Just a minute," said Snowy. "I'm a little slow at typing, you know, due to the fact that I don't have fingers."

Snowy continued tapping at the computer with the hoof pick: `cat nap.`

"OK," said Snowy. "Sorry about that. What was your question?"

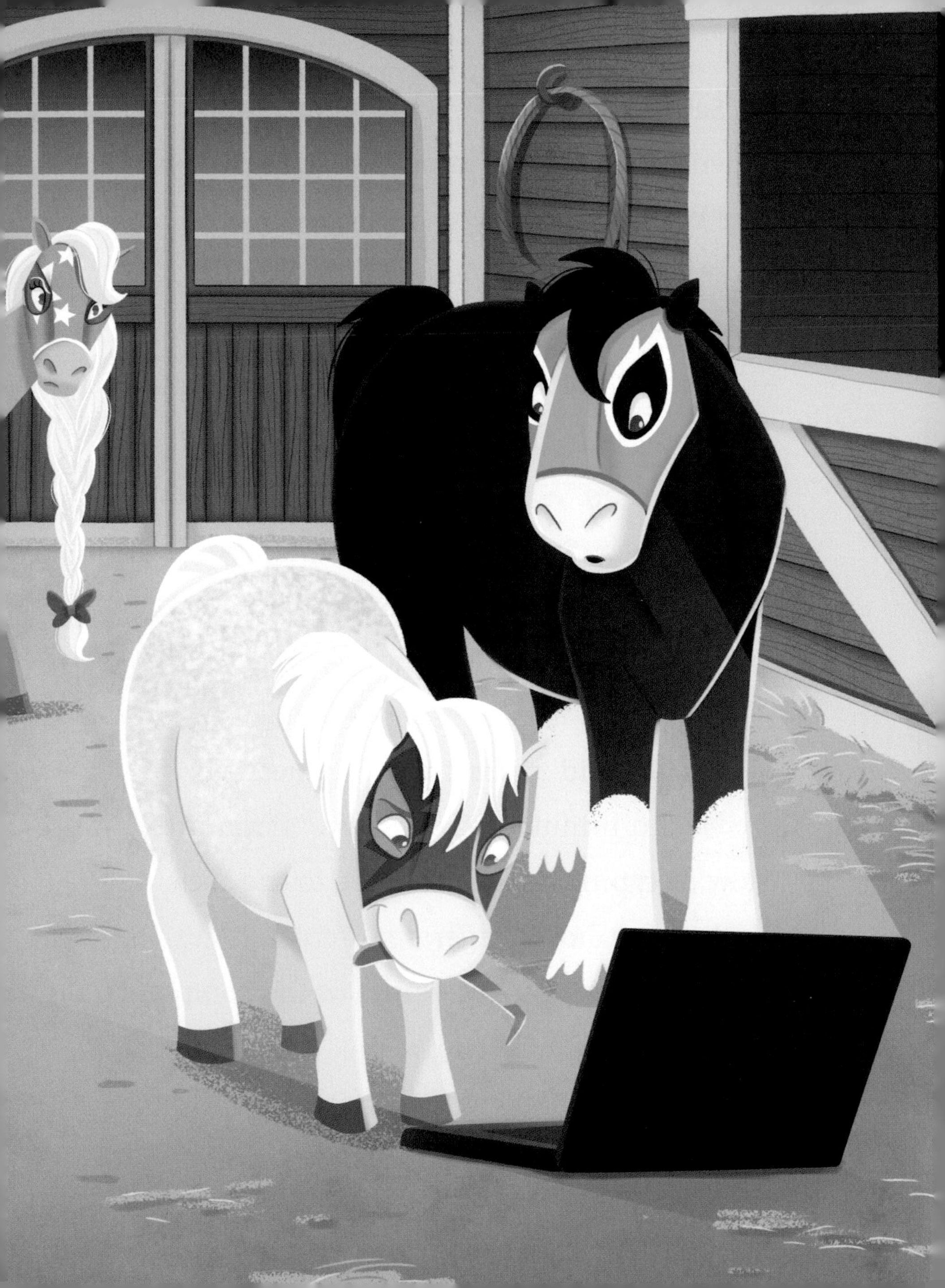

Seb stared at Snowy. Who ever heard of a typing pony? "Where did you get that pick?" asked Seb again.

"I spotted it on the desk the other day, so I stashed it behind the door," said Snowy. "I thought a laptop would be useful for writing my novel."

And that was good enough for Seb.

"Sebastian," said Snowy, tucking the hoof pick in his mask, "what do you want to do? Where do you want to go?"

Seb knew what he wanted to do. But he wasn't sure he wanted to tell Snowy yet. He thought it best to answer with a plain kind of answer—the kind of answer that would reveal nothing of his secret dream. "Find a clover field," he said.

Snowy took out his hoof pick and typed: clover field. "Anything else?" he asked.

Seb took a deep breath. It was his chance. His face turned red underneath his mask (as red as a horse's face can get). He pawed the ground. Nope. He couldn't say it. It wasn't the right time.

Seb turned to Snowy and quickly changed the subject. "And what about you?" he asked.

"I need to find a library," said Snowy.

CHAPTER 5

The Big Dark Something

Tres Caballos Incognito agreed to a plan:

- Stop by the big clover field. Eat some clover.
- Keep watch while Princess hunts and takes a cat nap.
- Find the library.

Seb quietly opened the barn door. It was dark outside. Snowy trotted out first. He inhaled deeply.

"Ah!" he said. "Can't you just smell it?"

Princess sniffed the ground. "Smell what?" she asked.

"The smell of adventure!" said Snowy.

Snowy trotted to the end of the driveway.

Princess slinked toward the maple tree to look for squirrels.

Seb did not move.

"What are you waiting for?" called Snowy. "Let's go!"

"Everything looks different in the dark," said Seb. "What if something gets me?"

"Nothing will get you," said Snowy.

"How do you know?" asked Seb.

"I just do," said Snowy. "Let's go!"

Seb trotted out in high alert mode. His head was high. His eyes darted everywhere, looking for something that might get him. Then he saw it—a Big Dark Something! And it was over by Princess!

"Princess!" he yelled. "Watch out! There is a Big Dark Something by you!"

Princess jumped. She looked around.

Then she saw it. The Big Dark Something was right next to her!

She tried to run, but she was frozen with terror. "Help me!" she cried.

Sebastian wouldn't budge. He was more of a scaredy-cat than Princess. The rescue mission was left to Snowy. He carefully walked sideways to Princess. As he walked, he stayed as far away from the Big Dark Something as possible. When he reached her, he took a hold of her long mane and started to lead her away.

Just then, the wind picked up. A plastic bag blew at Snowy.

"AHHHHH!" he yelled as he accidentally ripped Princess' bow. But as he galloped away, he headed straight toward the Big Dark Something. His hoof hit it. He jumped back, terrified. "The Something!" he screamed, closing his eyes, expecting the worst.

But nothing happened. The Big Dark Something did not bite. Or yell. Or move. In fact, the Big Dark Something did nothing.

Snowy gingerly touched it with his hoof again. Again, nothing.

"Wait a minute," said Snowy. He took off his mask and looked closer. Then he laughed.

"It's a tree stump!" he said. "The Big Dark Something is a tree stump!"

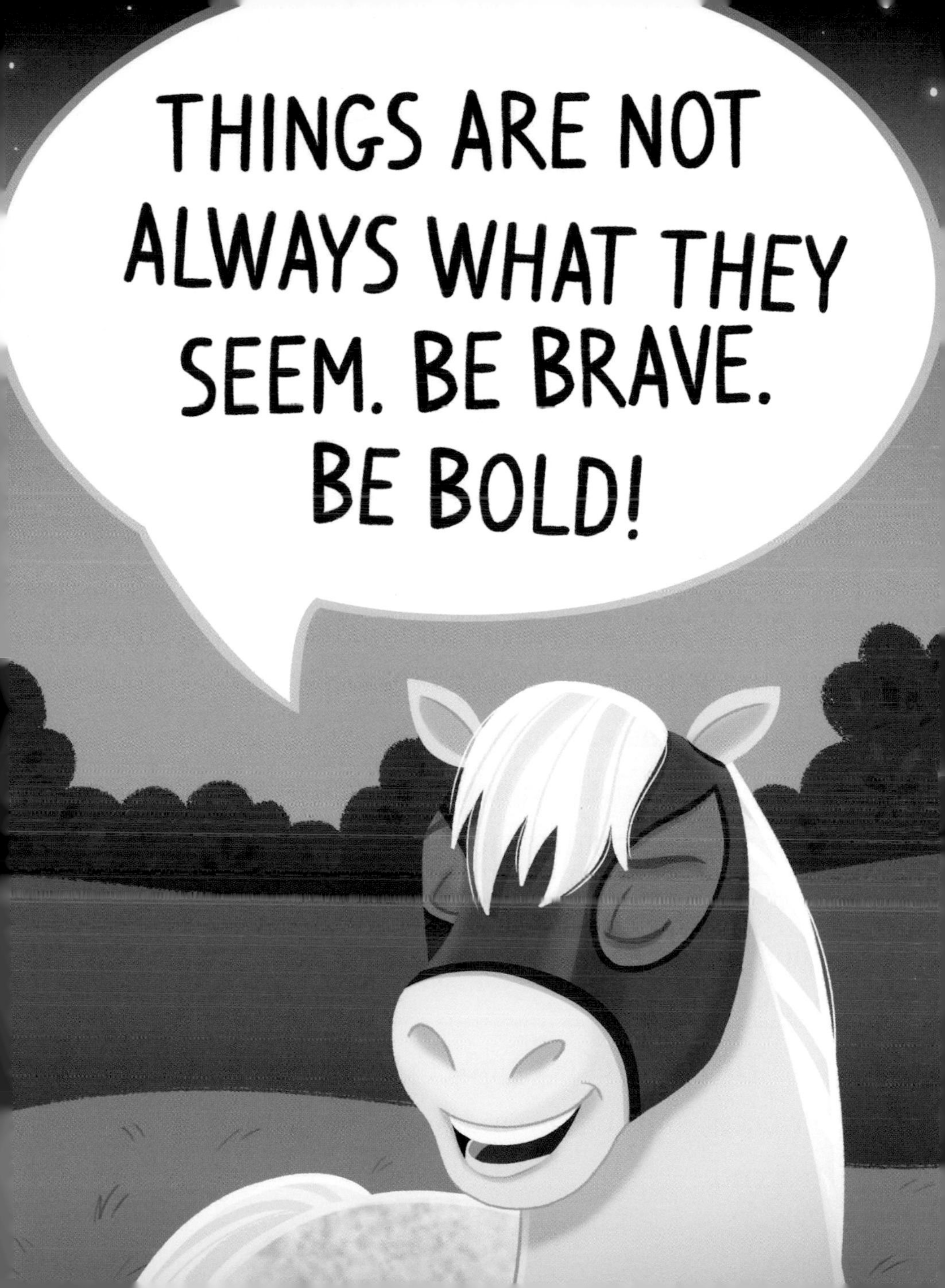
THINGS ARE NOT ALWAYS WHAT THEY SEEM. BE BRAVE. BE BOLD!

CHAPTER 6

The Clover Field

Soon the friends were trotting down the road, away from Farley Farms. They stopped a short way up the road at the big clover field. Seb was so happy that he ran in circles until he was out of breath. Then he bent his long neck and started to graze.

"This is the best," he said between mouthfuls. "We never get clover in our hay back at home."

"This is a perfect place to hunt," said Princess, sniffing around, eager to pick up a scent.

Snowy munched a bit. Then he got out his computer and hoof pick and typed:

```
Our hero was brave and bold.
He emerged from the shadows and
rescued the poor helpless creature.
The villain was petrified and retreated
into the darkness.
```

"Look!" said Princess. "A squirrel!"

The squirrel chattered at the group, and then it ran away.

Princess galloped after it.

The squirrel ran up a tree.

Princess reared and pawed up at the squirrel.

"Pooh," she said. "If I could just get up into the tree."

Seb looked up and smiled. "Well, cats do climb trees."

"That's true," said Princess, as she tried to climb up the trunk.

"This is much harder than it looks," she said. "Seb, Snowy, come here. Come help me. They've had me locked in that barn for so long. I must have forgotten how to climb a tree! I probably look pathetic!"

"You have no idea," said Seb under his breath.

"What did you say?" asked Princess.

"Nothing," Snowy interrupted. "He was talking about the clover. We'll be right over."

Seb looked at Snowy. "We will?" he asked.

"Of course," said Snowy. "It's the least we can do."

Snowy bent down so Princess could use him as a stepping stool to get onto Seb's back.

"Ouch!" said Seb as Princess' horseshoes dug into his head.

"I'm almost there!" said Princess.

The squirrel chattered away as Princess struggled to get her front legs up over the first branch.

"There you go!" said Snowy, "Now just use your back leg to push off Sebastian's head, and you will be in the tree!"

"I think you're both taking this cat thing too far," said Seb.

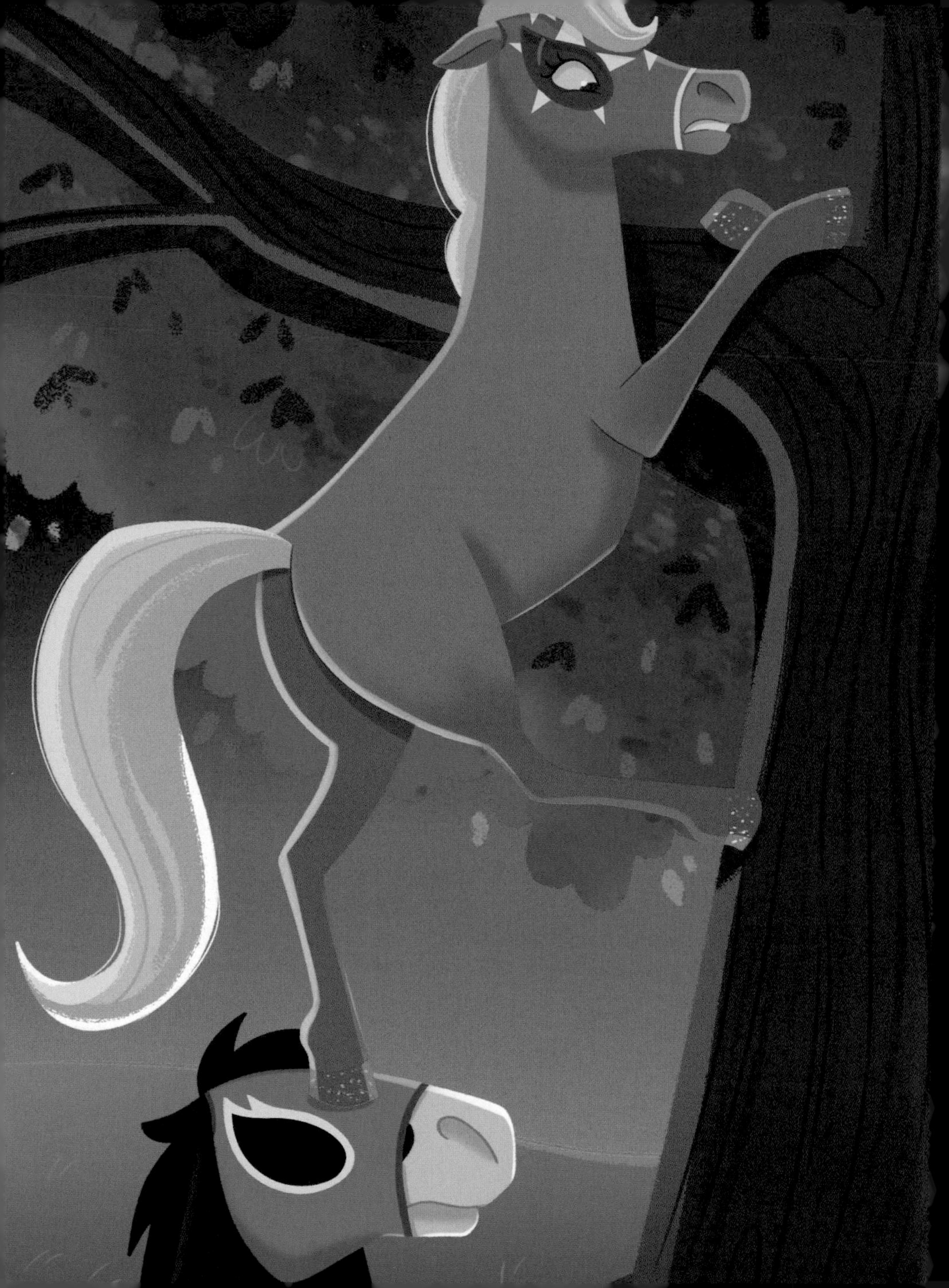

"Sebastian," said Snowy, "haven't you ever had a dream?"

Seb sighed. He knew about dreams. He closed his eyes and dug in his hooves. "OK, Princess," he said. "Just try to be a tender-footed kitty."

"Of course!" said Princess. "We cats are known to be lithe."

"Lithe?" asked Seb.

"That means graceful," said Snowy. And at that moment, Princess pushed all her weight right above Seb's eyes.

"OWWW!" yelled Seb.

"Whee!" said Princess. "Look at me! I'm in a tree!"

Princess tried to move toward the squirrel, but she couldn't. She was totally, 100%, unmistakably stuck!

CHAPTER 7

Stuck

"How embarrassing!" Princess said. "Here I am in the tree, and I can't even chase the squirrel!"

"Don't worry," said Snowy. "We will get you down!"

"Get me down?" huffed Princess. "I don't want to get down! I just got here. Just give me a minute to think about this. I'll figure it out."

"Fine with me," said Seb as he found a greener spot of clover on the far end of the field.

Snowy took out his computer and typed:

Just when our hero was on his way to
more exciting things, he got stuck. In
a tree. But not to worry, our hero—

"The Blizzard?" said Princess.

"Yes?" replied Snowy.

"Can you tell Melody that I found my true calling and that I plan to stay in this tree forever?" said Princess.

"Forever?" asked Snowy.

"Yes, forever," said Princess.

"That's a long time," said Snowy.

"Yes," said Princess. "But it's my destiny. I can feel it. It's heavenly up here. I can see for miles. Besides, I am finally doing what I was made to do."

"You were made to get stuck in a tree?" asked Snowy.

"No!" said Princess. "Chase squirrels! And catch them and eat them."

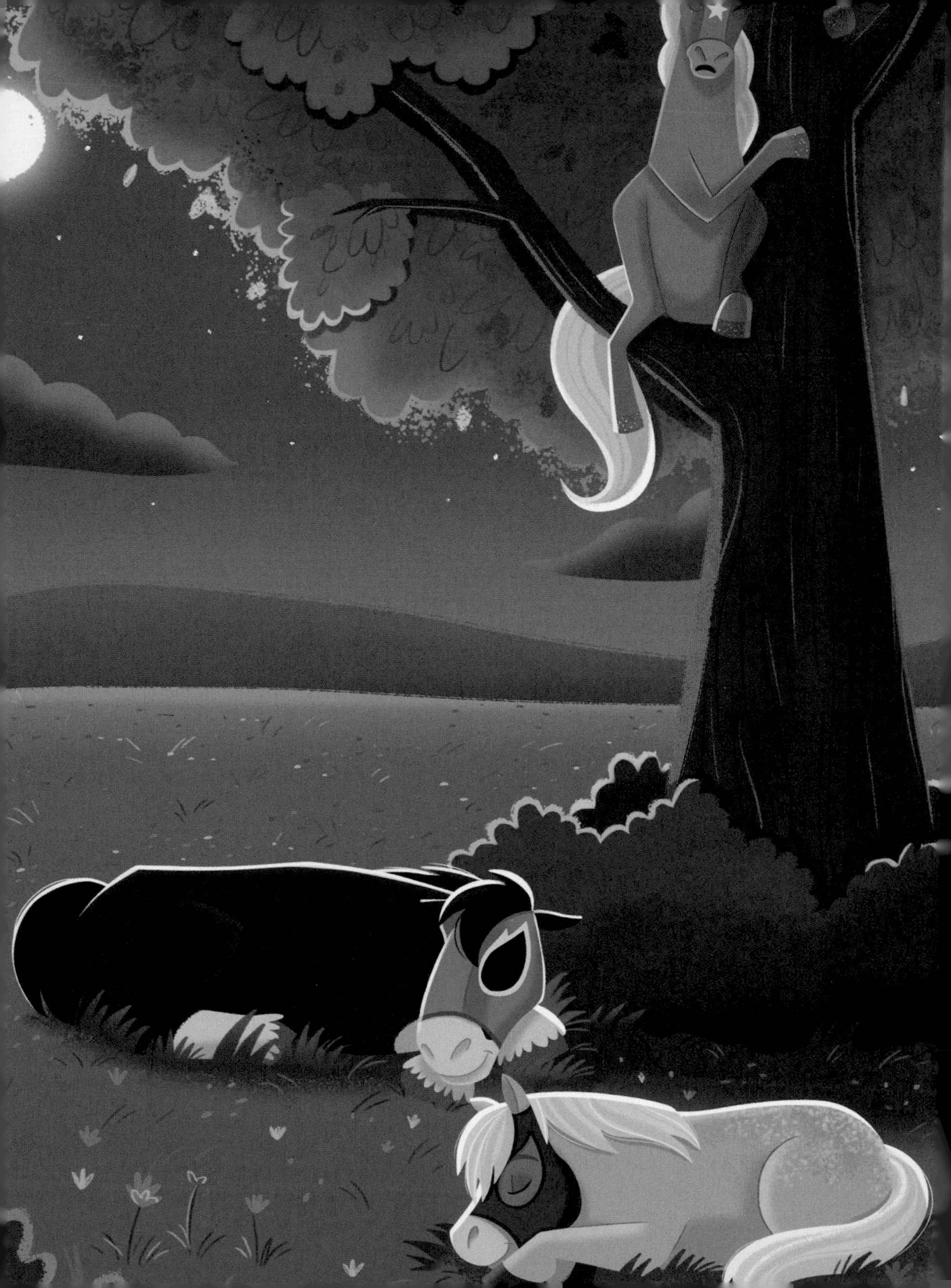

"Princess," said Snowy. "Please listen. I know you don't want to hear this, but I'm afraid you won't catch any squirrels when you are stuck like that."

"I'm only temporarily stuck. Cats are flexible. It won't be long, and I'll be running up that branch."

Princess tried to wiggle, but she didn't budge.

Snowy looked away and hoped she would admit her defeat soon. After all, he had to get to the library.

***

Princess didn't admit her defeat. Snowy knew he couldn't leave her there, so after they ate till they could eat no more, Seb and Snowy lay down under the tree and fell asleep.

CHAPTER 8

The Rescue

At dawn, Snowy woke to a fat squirrel sitting on his head. It was chattering. It was annoyed and wanted the horses to leave. Snowy shook his head, stretched, and got to his hooves.

Princess was crying.

"Are you ready to come down now?" asked Snowy.

"Yes," said Princess. "My tummy is growling and I didn't catch a squirrel. And I'm embarrassed to say, I'm still stuck."

Snowy nudged Seb. "Sebastian, it's time to wake up."

Seb stretched and yawned. He was not a morning horse.

"We need to help Princess," said Snowy.

Seb nuzzled his head on the soft dewy clover bed and closed his eyes. "Just tell her to jump," he mumbled.

Princess heard him. "I can't jump!" she cried. "What if I fall? What if I break a leg?" Princess was starting to panic.

"Calm down," said Snowy. "I'll think of something."

Snowy looked around. That's when he spotted it—a checkered bed sheet stuck between some bushes. It must have blown off a clothesline.

Snowy grabbed the sheet with his teeth. He gently nudged Seb. "Sebastian, hold this, please!"

Seb grudgingly held one end of the sheet in his teeth. Snowy took the other.

"Think of it as a trampoline," said Snowy. "Jump. We'll catch you."

Princess looked down. "I've never been on a trampoline," she said.

"You haven't?" asked Snowy.

"No," she said. "Have you?"

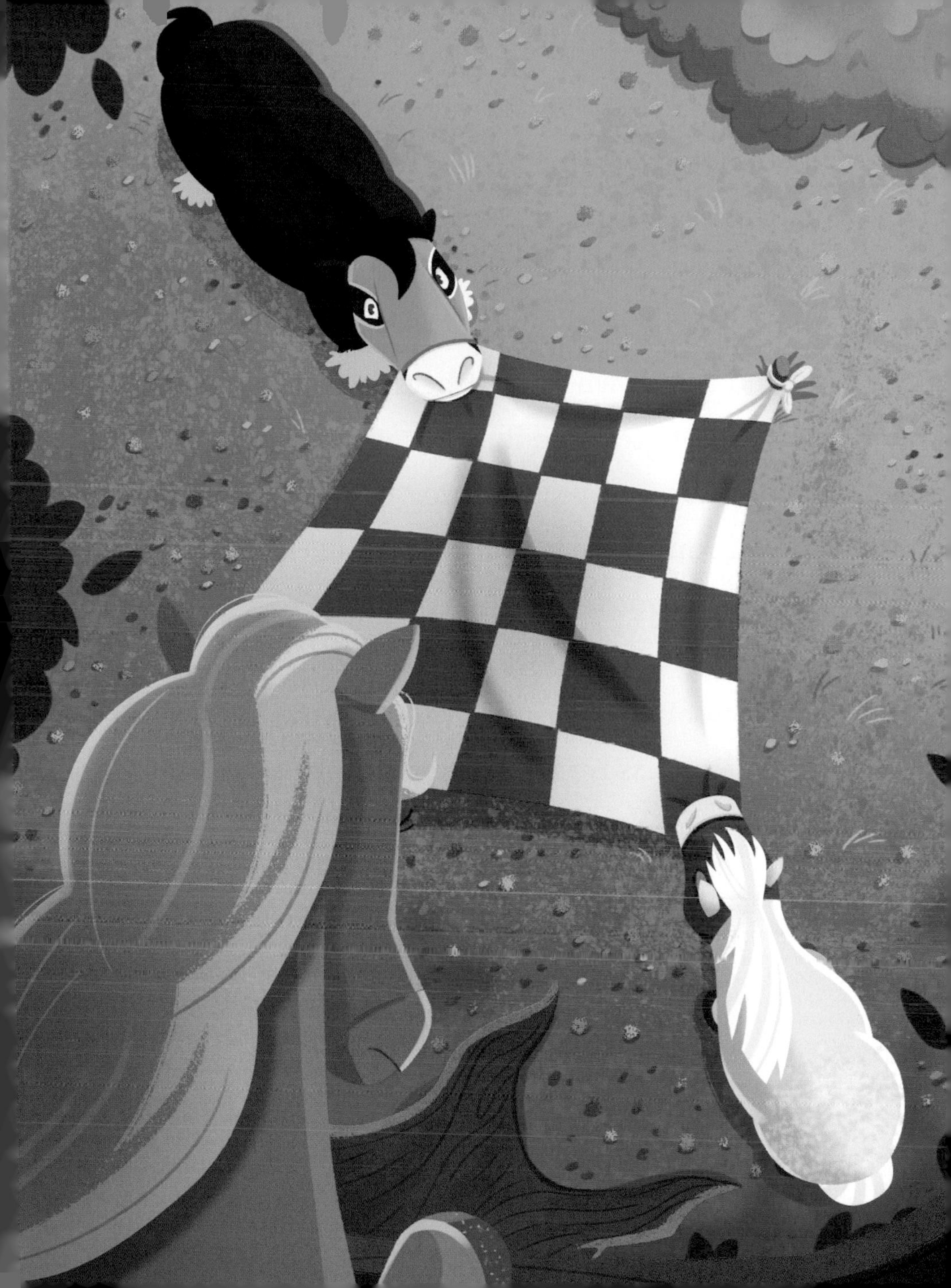

"Well, not exactly," said Snowy. "But it's not a big deal. You can do it."

Princess looked at the sheet. It seemed to be a long, long way down. She cried in terror. "No!!!!"

And that is when Toni heard them. Princess screamed so loud, Toni could hear her all the way over at Farley Farms.

Toni ran right over. "What on earth?" she asked scratching her head.

A few minutes later, she returned with the tractor and a special crane and carefully picked Princess from the tree.

CHAPTER 9

Back at the Barn

Back at the barn, Toni prepared some bran mash for the horses.

"I'm still not sure how you all got out of your stalls or how Princess got in a tree," she said shaking her head. "And what's with the fly masks? Were they some sort of disguise or something?"

Princess nudged her stall door and nodded her head.

"Well," she said, patting each of them on the neck, "you had quite the adventure, but I'm glad you are all back safe and sound."

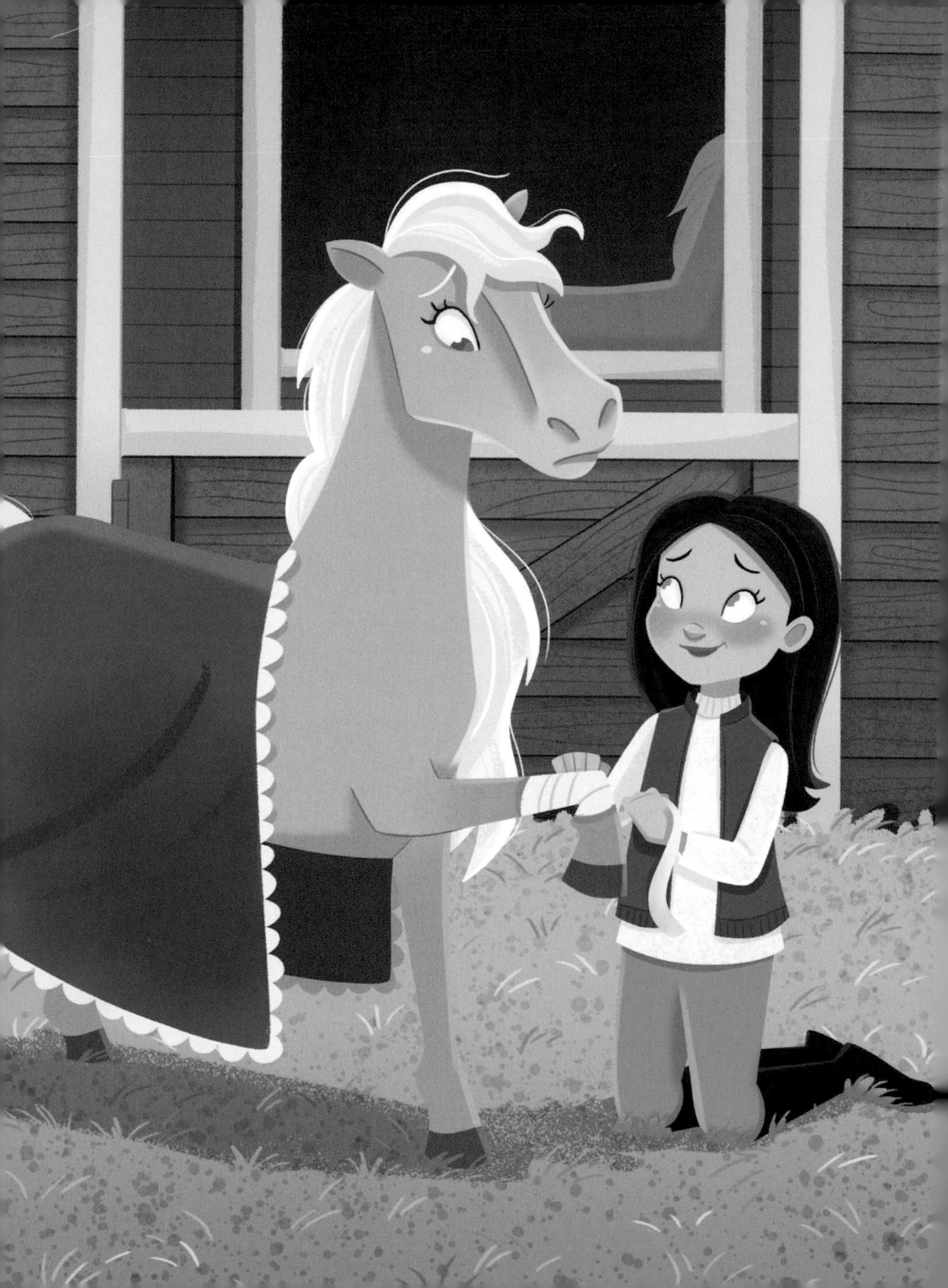

Just then, Melody opened the barn door. "Prin-cesssssss!" she called. "Are you ready for the show?"

The show!

Princess had forgotten all about it.

When Melody saw Princess—her messy mane and a giant scrape on her leg—she became hysterical. "Oh! My poor baby! What happened?" asked Melody.

Princess laid her head against Melody.

"My sweet girl," said Melody checking every inch of her horse. "You're a mess. But I'm glad you're not too hurt."

Melody looked at the barn clock and sighed. "There's not enough time to get you cleaned up and ready for the show today," she said. "We'll have to miss this one."

Melody brushed Princess, tended her wound, and wrapped her in a pink blanket.

Princess nickered softly as her eyes started to close.

The three horses rested for the remainder of the day. But later that night, they started thinking about their next escape.

"It was awfully nice getting out of the barn," said Seb.

"And I never did catch that squirrel," said Princess.

"And I still need more material for my novel," said Snowy.

"Where should we go next?" they all said at once.

GLOSSARY

clover—a small, leafy plant that grows low to the ground

criticize—to point out the good and bad in others

defeat—when a person has lost at something

disgust—a strong feeling of dislike

feline—any animal of the cat family

fly mask—a mask used to protect a horse's eyes and jaw from flies

gingerly—very carefully

humiliate—to make someone look or feel foolish

hysterical—unable to control emotions

inspect—to look at something carefully

mission—a planned job or task

pathetic—weak or useless

terror—very great fear

ABOUT THE AUTHOR

Cari Meister has written more than 130 books for children, including the Tiny series (Penguin) and the Fast Forward Fairy Tales series (Scholastic). Cari is a school librarian and she loves to visit other schools and libraries to talk about the joy of reading and writing. Cari lives in the mountains of Colorado with her husband, four boys, one horse, and one dog.

ABOUT THE ILLUSTRATOR

Heather Burns is an illustrator from a small town called Uttoxeter in the UK. In 2013, she graduated from the University of Lincoln with a degree in illustration and has been working as a freelance illustrator ever since. Heather has a passion for bringing stories to life with pictures and hopes that her work makes people smile. When she's not working she's usually out walking her grumpy black Labrador, Meadow!

TALK ABOUT IT

1. What do you think Seb was going to tell Snowy on page 28?

2. What do you think was going through Snowy's mind when he went to rescue Princess from the Big Dark Something?

3. Pretend Princess thinks she's a dog instead of a cat. How would that change the story?

WRITE ABOUT IT

1. What do you think Seb was thinking while Princess was stuck in the tree? Rewrite the scene from his point of view.

2. Write about a fourth horse to join *Tres Cabellos Incognito*. What does it look like? What's its name?

3. Write about what would have happened if Toni hadn't rescued Princess from the tree. Do you think Snowy's plan would have worked?

BOOKS IN THE THREE HORSES SERIES

THE FUN DOESN'T STOP HERE!